I0566463

" *Love & Life*

Made Into

Poetry"

by

Crystal Davison

Davison Publishing - Cypress, Texas

www.crystaldavison.com

Printed in the United States of America

ISBN 978-0-9761150-4-5

Collection of Poems

Poetry

Dedication

I dedicate this book to my beautiful friends

who have supported my life, dreams, and

aspirations from childhood:

Johanna, Katrina, Gloria, & Aza.

You have been the best hand picked family.

Thank you for everything!

Message to my Readers:

Thank you for taking time out of your life

to acknowledge my work.

I am truly thankful and honored.

Angels of the Sky

Just woke up beginning my new day

Outside the window flew a bird and sat on a small tree

While sitting I laid my eyes on he

Paused into time,

it had captured me.

That little sparrow made me smile inside,

Its sight

had kissed the very spirit of me.

Love's Rhapsody

He is my Jimi Hendrix –

With no guitar

and no voice for song.

Just his rhythmic

soulful silence

that plays for me

colorful vibrant music,

in my heart beats.

Endless Love

I'm in love with the matter of you

Down to the atoms of you

Back to the Adams of you.

So in love,

In this lifetime not enough time with you

Can't get enough of you

I hope I'm blessed to live through infinite

eternity with you

Breathe in all the air from which you are through

Let me count the ways.

You soothe me

Time's measure dissolves in the arms of you

There is no need of things to do

Heavenly is the silence with you

My soul's ultimate rest is the presence of you

Saying I do

Can't justify my love for you

I want to shout into every day my soul has found its

truce

Walk in any and every direction with you

No other in existence will ever do

I want to reside in the soul of you

A true crown has been won

in this lifetime to have lived

and shared a love such as you.

Genesis

Godly man

approaches Godly woman,

now that's a story

with all the glory.

He'll discuss head in terms of the direction

he envisions our lives to go in.

He'd decline only wanting a piece of me,

but desiring me in whole mind, body, and soul.

The missing piece should only be to complete his life,

And if he goes into her she becomes his rib,

One body,

One flesh,

One soul.

Saints Love

Hi newness,

bye bye oldness,

patience has been my virtue.

So many seasons have gone by

with many new lessons learned.

I'm ready to give love a new try.

New steps taken by faith

without sight.

Happy once again

I'm awake dancing in the light.

I am awake in living color

I'm dancing in the light.

Aligned in time,

arrived are you & I.

Aligned by the divine

to extend his royal line.

I knew you had arrived

as I felt you provide,

my surely divined,

very last

"first kiss."

Forever Mine

We come from different places

But we have arrived into the same moment

Now that I have you

I don't want to exist into another day

without you.

Beastly Love

I want to be loved by a beast,

Held by a beast.

Where only I am his beauty,

I am who he looks to

in this world to see,

And he loves

only me.

My Infinity

I'd watch him to see how he allows GOD

to guide his steps on the earth

as he walks confidently in the way

that he should go.

I'd listen for his voice to speak in truth,

with integrity,

and fruitfully

to all branches

keeping him connected to the vine.

I'd watch for how he looks at me

and know that he is intensely

working with GOD

to love me under no specific conditions

for a lifetime

into eternity.

I'd watch how he touched me

in protective gentleness

as I have become an extension of him

and his lineage of GOD

under this sun.

The very kiss of him

makes me close my eyes

to small glimpses into heaven's

realm here on earth,

I desire

for eternity.

Eternally Yours

Your love feels 1,000 years strong already,

Thank you for your love,

Thank you for your kindness,

Thank you for your respect,

Thank you for your time,

Thank you for allowing me

to feel loved without any conditions,

for all of time.

Divine

It's been a long race through time,

Our ancestors have passed us the torch.

May I have this moment to stare into your eyes

and walk slow with you

for

just

a

little

while,

Witness your divine,

through your touch.

True Love

Life happens …

Things fall apart,

And love cannot pick up all the pieces.

All those pieces *can remain broken*,

but love will be the golden token.

It will sustain you through

and create a new you.

It remains in the origination of you.

And as change happens over and over to you,

that love will remain the same.

With you I find silence.

With you time has no essence.

With you I find joy.

With you I have resilience.

There is nothing I can't go through with love provided
by you.

When I fail I have you.

When I win I have you.

When I gain I have you.

When I lose I have you.

You evolve your love to engulf

all that I ever become.

Your love is strong,

its presence is in the air I want to breathe.

It feels atomic.

And I always feel you with me.

No one can bring me down

because you keep me so lifted up.

I walk with such an overflow,

I have enough to share with others.

Thank you for your love.

Thank you for your presence.

Thank you for your resilience.

Thank you for something amazingness,

I can't even imagine I deserve.

Thank you for being the definition

of a thing called true love.

Thankful Love

Saying "I love you"

isn't good enough

to express the depth of how I feel.

I just thank GOD for you.

Forever Yours

I betcha didn't see me coming,

Coming into your life

to love

you forever.

Unconditionally,

Without the returned favor,

Forever.

Wanted

If you are here to break my heart,

Please do

and hurry up.

If you are here to love me like crazy,

Please do

and I want you to hurry it up.

If you are here to take me beyond my wildest dreams,

I want you to

and please speed it up.

If you are here to do nothing but comfort me softly

through the world's pains,

I want that too.
I surrender,

just please hurry up.

Till Death Do Us Part

I don't care about your flaws,

as long as they don't affect me

I don't care about your lies,

and long as you share the truth with me

I don't care what you assume about things,

until you have confirmed them with me

I don't care what others think,

because they are not Jesus

who remains the center of our marriage and all things

No human can break the Godly union

he has put in place for you and me,

those that do attempt are ungodly demonic beings

Protect your ears from unGodly beings

Guard your heart as it dictates all of your being

We must protect our marriage

and it's not based on these worldly views of things

Our actions are our unspoken words

Our words start and end in our vows

Our words should flow from that of the godly olive tree

Corinthians love for one another,

is the only heavenly place on earth we share
unfathomably

with one another until the last breaths of we

Our home is our sanctuary,

we must protect it righteously

No one comes before you,

as you have seen

Nothing comes before you,

as you have seen

Let's fight together every demonic thought,

do not let them consume thee

I ask that you wake from the realm of uncertainty

and lean on Jesus Christ

with all trust & faith in he.

Know that I stand unmovable as your wife,

against all battles we encounter

until the death of you or me.

I Choose You Babe

You are not the man

of my dreams

but better

Because

You are the man

of my reality,

My everything.

ADtom

I desire the very Adtom's of you

To create more abundant life

through me.

Soul Glow

Here I go again

Peeling back thy skin,

And revealing thy soul

For you.

Crazy in Love

It's like the truth is hiding a lie right?

And the lies is hiding the truth all the time.

They seem well together,

or not.

But people stay

trying to pull them apart.

From the start

There's no point minding

To the heart,

That's truly in love.

The Blessing

I pray that as man and woman

You unite into a marriage gracefully

Blessed within the covenant of GOD.

May your yesterdays,

todays,

tomorrows,

and promised eternity,

be firm in your sure strength of oneness,

Starting today.

Perfectly Imperfect

Too good to be true

But I deserve you

And you deserve me

You want a future with me

And I want all the days of my life with you

It's where we have found our contentment

It's our blessed love to keep

We will work for it.

Sustain it.

Protect it.

And our love will remain ours -perfectly imperfect

for us

It's our complete.

Hiding our imperfections deep down inside

Let them shine their lights and dissect it all-

we have nothing to hide

Maybe we do?

Maybe we don't?

Maybe we both want to avoid all those truths.

Maybe you tell me all of yours

Maybe I'll tell you all of mine

... Those things the past has done to us

... All those things the past has embedded in us

Will remain our integrity.

Because -

It makes everything different about us change

if we take those imperfections away.

It breaks our unique craft as one perfectly timed mold

perfect

for one another.

Our love for one another is a perfection creator.

We are a perfectly imperfect love

like them all,

And complete.

Adorn

My favorite moments...

When I close my eyes

And I anticipate what I can't see

Then I reach out

And my fingertips

touch thee

... And I feel

that you are real.

A lightning blitz.

Every time,

it's like a granted wish

... for me.

To have you

Every day

My little moments

of ecstasy

I desire

You forever more.

Here and Now

Don't forget

to love me today,

As if there

is no tomorrow.

Grateful Love

I just wanted to say "thank you" today,

for the things I can't acknowledge

or appreciate of you *today*.

But in the future on some days,

I will know

I should have

said "thank you"

in so many yesterdays.

Needed You

I went into the world

and got myself hurt

I didn't wait patiently for you

like I should have

Now you're spending time

healing me

Looking for where it hurts

You finally found me

Closing the wounds

I've caused you

before we met.

Needed Love

Love is like water

They operate kinda the same

How they both come and go

So vital

that my hands can't hold on to you.

Uncontrollable,

Calculated to uncalculatable.

Necessary,

Magnificent.

Deadly without them.

Beautiful,

Super naturals,

I need and desire them both.

Dear Future Love

I suppose once you find me

I'll still cry

about the days before,

when I lived without you

And your redeeming type

of love.

Melting for You

Our solid existence finds one another
Communicates through the silence
Our souls whisper
Through the world's existence
An internal spiritual brilliance

is sparked that can't be seen,

but I can feel it.
And it feels good despite the world's resilience.
Transcending time and space without stillness.
I am trapped,

I submit to this feeling.
Unviewable by eyes,

no one can see
The negotiated aligned desire

of our souls gyrating together

before our pitched words to one another

into reality.

Like fire burning inside of ice...

but no drip.

We haven't even touched yet,

let me look into your eyes again

for that futuristic glimpse.

Quietly I am held hostage to captivity,

I submit.

I want so desperately what I can feel as reality.

I want to explore more of the rush

bottled inside of me.

Letting go no longer holding ice cold..

When we lock eyes once again,

I will show signs I'm melting you,

I'll let go.

Never Leave my Side

You left you,

to be with me.

I left me,

to be with you.

Let's dance

through this time

and space in the now

into forevers,

as one.

I Need You

How many days until I find thee?

How many days do I have to wake up,

put on makeup.

And walk here,

and sit there,

and dance here,

and laugh at that,

and attend this,

and be there,

Until you find me?

How many days until I find thee,

Let me continue counting the days.

Broken Leaps

Why do some escape

and abandon who they are,

To attach to the easiest found things

for love.

My Love

I don't want to tolerate you,

I want to love you,

I want to like you,

I want to look forward to seeing you,

I want to miss when you are gone.

Priceless

Big house filled with fancy things-

all peace and no love.

Little house filled with broken things-

some peace and overwhelmed with love.

Which house do you choose?

Now you play the judge-

What is the price for a hug?

What is the price to be born

and end up paying for love?

Majestically

He creates a clear way

for two specific things

to run smash

into one another,

in this whole wide

entire universe.

Then...

Together they disseminate,

Or die,

or grow into full life

with one another.

Choosey Lover

Tho they have no other,

Alone they are in this life

And in the same space

without the need

or desire for one another,

A choice.

Dream Catcher

To have any regrets means,

I also forfeit all the perfect moments

that I am thankful for,

and have shared with you.

Promise

Someone said,

"Happiness doesn't choose you,

you have to choose it,"

So then I revealed my love for you,

now you have to grasp

the reality of it.

Patiently I'll wait.

Perfectly Crossed Paths

In the wrong time,

I could have met you a thousand times

and naturally walked away.

But because I spent a thousand days with you,

I grew closer,

And became wiser.

Now I can meet you

a thousand times,

and each time be grateful

and desire you

to stay.

Please Try Harder

I know that you love me back,

I need for you to trust me back.

I Choose Me

I want to be your type

But I need to be my own type

of person.

Stairway to Heaven

No matter how much I make other people laugh,

Nothing's funny to me

Who bothers to make me laugh?

No matter how much I love others,

Nobody is loving me back

I'm giving and they're taking.

I'm reaching but nothing's there.

I have me, and me, and then me.

And I know I am built for this,

But it's killing me.

Can I go back please

Back now-

to heaven please.

568 Days

Coming from behind the bars...

Of a broken heart

For it's the worst mental prison.

Gone Baby

When something that meant everything to you,

now means nothing.

Brokenhearted

Somebody dim the sun

And make it go back to night

I'm not ready

I'm not ready

I am todays fool,

who wants to stay out of sight.

Good Luck

You are perfect in every way

But not what I want.

Desired Trouble

... It's like a drug.

They call it romantic love

Can introduce you to real "trouble"

Have you hypnotized

Then leave your soul vandalized

To seek its feeling

It's false healing

In a world of sizzling pain

Lurking at every corner

Hiding are you

Seeking that feeling

You take that quick fix

That quick sexual healing

Wake up wake up wake up wake up

It's not love tonight.

Deep pain deep pain deep pain deep pain

Wrong don't care for right.

And when those nights end

And when romantic love vanished out of sight

Reality is in the view

Again there is you.

Its ashes are too little remnants

Left to understand.

To pick up and go on in life

Now who are you?

You ask yourself

After another self inflicted burn.

Some survive

It's the worst fire dive

Changes the whole path of your life

Saved may be you

Once you realize

It was you who covered your real eyes

to enjoy real lies in dark pockets of the world

While getting tired of waiting on real light.

Real light...

Was always in plain sight.

Closer

You lead me on,

then pushed me away.

You'd turn me off,

But-

bring me back closer

with the right words to say.

Loved me right,

Until you got what you needed.

Left me all alone,

until I was once again

what you needed.

Yearning for You

Dying inside

Trying to hide

My addicted insides

for you.

Calm outside

my soul cries inside

Trying to shake the thoughts of life

I want with you.

I close my eyes,

in our old memories I try to reside

while quenching heartaches inside,

Because I don't have you.

Jump In With Both Feet

It doesn't matter how deep the water is,

You just need to know how to swim.

In love,

You won't know what the circumstances will be,

You just need to know how to love.

Lighthouse

While you were so busy

Watching me,

I was watching you

You forgot to watch yourself,

Now you are adrift

And un-shored

Without ship.

Damaged Goods

Because of you,

I can't imagine trusting again

Even though,

I can imagine loving again.

Stole

I asked nothing of you,

You took everything from me.

You Already Walked Away

Why you keep checking in

Is it the right thing to do?

Who are you checking in for?

Me or you?

Trying to keep one foot in the door

Don't worry about my feelings no more

When's the right time to come back,

you just might

Not sure if your choice was right?

Do you want to know when things are going more
perfectly right?

Let's make one point clear

One thing I know for sure is *we* or *things*

Will never be perfect enough

for you to come back to my dear.

Sometimes

Bad choices vs. desperate choices

For love.

I Can't Do This

How do I?

When do I?

Know...

to walk away.

Unbreak My Heart

But I'm still alive.

I feel my heart beats.

And I love you,

But don't have you.

I feel me breathing.

My eyes can see everything before me.

But why?

Make it all stop.

Blank me out,

Now.

No you.

I don't want

me.

Pay Attention

I surrendered to love,

shame on me.

I found out I surrendered

to nothing but an illusion,

shame on me.

Open heart

As I am faced daily

with reasons not to love you,

May I work even harder

to discover reasons

to continue loving you.

Choices

I will learn you with patience,

I will do my part to make us last.

I will love you to death,

But I will leave you fast.

I know that love is a humans

most highest experience,

I know that GOD must be the center,

as he will protect and guide me through it.

I know that in life

we will go through our seasons.

I know that there is no season to stay,

if pain has become the only reason

we last.

Destined

The heart wants

what the heart wants

in the world.

But the spirit seeks

that which is equally yoked,

For its duty,

into eternity.

Blurred Vision

I hope that when I finally realize it,

You will still be standing here,

Within reach.

Save Me

Why don't I scream?

I'm not living a dream

This feels like a nightmare

And I can't stare the truth in the face.

I'm a coward right now.

Things are scaring me.

I'm not as courageous as I thought I was.

This is forcing me to live in a new reality.

How do I get inside that thing called a dream.

It only seems…

Like its words.

And I'm stuck

Without much.

Cause I'm only human.

And GOD's timing is my resolve.

Chosen

You left me alone

for dead

But by the love of thee

Look at me now,

HE always shows

he had plans for me.

Ashes to Ashes

Dead and gone

Ashes are the memories

I live on-

With your love,

Rotted in the chest of me.

Lost and Found

Some days you will be lost,

and some days you will be found.

These rarely happen

on the same day.

Times Thief

I was used by you,

I was all that you needed.

I realize it was never about me,

But the sustaining of you that you needed.

You told me you loved me,

Maybe because I was the only one always there.

To consume the time of another person's life

on behalf of yourself,

is that fair?

Ready to Love Again

You lit my candle after it had been blown out.

You made my spirit smile and see the light again

after it had been hidden from the world in the dark,

and no longer wanted to come out.

I heard the music again,

the past mental scenes

and voices that had been holding me

captive to the past finally drowned out.

You gave me a glimpse of love

that I could once again envision for myself

and never wanted to be without.

Distant Lovers

It hurts to be with you.

It hurts to be without you.

I feel like I'm dying

Though no tear has dropped.

All day my soul is crying,

Yearning for you.

I'm dodging where I know you will be

As I am lost until I find you.

Why does it feel like I can't go on?

I've mentally re-weathered all those seasons of our love,

I've investigated all the reasons we righteously went
wrong.

And I know that we can't work,

And I know that we can work.

But in this silence it tells me,

I'm still alone.

This silent separation tells me

I'm the only one who wants for us to go on.

Why does it have to be this way?

I say nothing to you and everything to me,

as it's been in the equation

why our love has slowly dissolved away.

And in the equation

of the expectations of me I found in your eyes-

but never heard from your lips,

slowly dissolved our love away.

Together in the silence

is where our love always felt the strongest.

Silence to our future.

Silence to our love.

Our love like others' ...

Has been created and now lost in time.

Royalty

I stand alone because I do not trust

my heart with someone who has to live in today's
society.

I stand alone because I do not trust

my spirit to be intertwined

and lead by one who is not led by GOD alone,

I want royalty from the kingdom

who is here in the world but not of the world,

by yoke of thy throne.

New Day

Willing

And devoted

HE and I

I and He

Come hand in hand

Ready

As one

Through the odds

To fight

the generational curse

With His power in thee.

Roller Coaster

Pity the sincere lovers,

For such a roller coaster of emotions

life will become.

Hang on tight

Because the loops, spins, skips, and drops

Will truly

never ever end,

Hang tight.

Check Mate

Uh oh,

You are not playing the game right

You suppose to keep your feelings to yourself.

I'm gonna have to move around

...since you got that look in your eyes

My queue

to escape.

Fourth Quarter

Why you just can't play the game fair?

Can you pick up those flowers off the field?

Can you reach and grab all those hearts out the air?

We don't play like that around here.

You need to go back to the sidelines

and watch the game played again.

You gotta keep your feelings to yourself.

New Start

I got a brand new dress

for a man I ain't met yet.

I got some brand new shoes

to wear with it too.

I sing out loud excitedly proud,

"I'm new to the market."

Pretty Please

I like who you are

as a person.

And I would like to be a part

of that which you are.

Add a part of my life to yours,

for I want to have more life with you

going forward.

No Strings Attached

I hate the feeling of being attached

to something and not wanting to let it go.

I love the feeling of being desired

more than I can ever know.

I open my mind, heart, and hands

to allow you to come and go.

Waiting for You

I wonder…

Was I your blessing or your curse?

Imagine right now that you are following my body

as I lay lifeless in a hearse,

My dear love I wonder

am I going in a plot that we picked out,

for you too will join me

returned to this dirt right by my side.

Like all, our love had its rifts

and I gathered I always loved you the most.

The Corinthians love I took for you

in our vows

will remain in me as I loved you

now, today, forever, and always.

Regardless of this dirt earth

Until you once join me again

in the heavenly clouds.

We Belong Together

If things fall apart,

May they always come back,

together.

In Due Season

Some people know how to fix things

when they are broken,

others do not.

Some people know how to stay dedicated

and give it all they got,

Until they reap

what they have so graciously sewn.

Float On

Drifting in

Checking out

Saving thyself is what's is all about

What is real?

What's is fake?

Mix it all together

... we all bake & taste our own fates

Love me now

What am I?

Who are we?

So much always feels at stake?

We wait everyday for the ending to see

...what eternal mysteries await.

Unseen

Your journey is bigger than this one day,

it's eternal.

GOD craft into your life has eternal effects,

nothing short term.

Don't get caught up on one event

or one day,

when you have an eternal journey ahead,

Stay your course

... and keep on staying

for new chapters that awaits.

Free Bird

I am free spirit,

I may be witnessed,

experienced,

but not captured.

My Friend

Thank you for listening

Thank you for not speaking

Thank you for caring

Thank you for just being there.

Relieved

I can't tell if I'm mad at you or me

I can't tell if I wish me dead

or so happy how alive I feel

with the truth set free.

Go Scarlett

March on...

Only GOD can judge you.

Beauty Seconds

Before my eyes

I am watching you grow.

While it is not pleasant to my eyes

I don't want to miss the best part,

Your finale

Into a great butterfly.

Rose in the Concrete

Grow with the resources you have,

and do not have.

As God will provide the *rest*.

I Am Strong

Are the trees complaining, or weathering the storm?

All things on earth go through it,

don't think for one moment

it's only happening to you.

Can the trees consider the days they withstand a storm?

Do they not grow wider stronger roots to hold ground?

Some trees are nicer looking than others

to the eyes of the beholder,

But does it matter, for they too stand sanctified?

All things have their own glory to God.

Beautiful is every tree after the storm,

Beautiful is all things that survive.

Please Let Me Go

I want to just give up trying ...

and try really really hard

all at the same time.

I want you

I want us

I need new

I need trust

I fear pain

So much to gain

I want to fight me for your love

I want to fall helplessly in love

History please let me go

History please let me go

You changed me

And now I'm changing things

make me some different kinds of memories

History the future needs me now

You done your works

please let me go

I've been changed in ways

he will never need to know,

history goodbye.

No Backpedaling

It's all good until you begin asking too many questions,

And getting too many answers.

The Movement

Are we still struggling,

Or you think it's all done?

You-

Got to keep it moving ,

"Sshhh, just like that!"

One

by

one.

Those history books are going to read:

"It was unpredictable, collectively, they infiltrated.

And now, the damage is done."

Vibes

It cannot be passed down to you,

It cannot be gained,

held on to or retained.

It comes and it goes.

True felt wealth is found

in the richness of the moments.

In the seconds of the minutes,

It awaits you.

Seek it,

Put yourself

in the presence of the people

and the places

where it is greatest felt

for you.

And feel it.

2015

A ship just sank with 800 people at sea,

200 girls were just rescued

who were held captive for a new religious diplomacy,

An earthquake just killed thousands in Nepal,

And riots over injustice to those of certain colors

are happening all over the world to time's uncertainties.

Today many will fall asleep

with broken hearts from all kinds of worries

Like the broken heart love has also given to me.

Through it all I remember

God has plans to prosper me,

Stay strong and be patient,

Revelation is soon near,

we all will see.

I Belong

If everybody is doing right,

then who is doing the wrong?

When your religion ain't my religion,

Your culture ain't my culture,

Your color ain't my color,

Your gender ain't my gender,

Now what?

Who is the judge?

Positive At Your Best

And you were expected to smile

in that photograph because...

When you do look back in time

It captured a moment in your life

At best you deemed

In that moment

You were aware

That you were alive.

Elevate

It's not attached to gravity,

It can transcend time.

I can feel how I want

I can leave the now moment

and go wherever.

It's not a secret

It's the best power granted ever

Visualize your future,

Then your actions catch you there

In reality

That catch is the best,

Ever.

Devoted Love

I wonder how many times she tried to walk away,

And how many years she dedicated of her life,

How many lonely nights,

How many disappointments,

How many things that just weren't right,

How many others,

How much of the truth she held onto and suffered,

How many times of embarrassment and shame,

How many times she had to justify,

How many times she tried to walk away,

How many times she heard the speech

As he looked her straight in the eyes,

How did she smile,

And love that man so dearly through all that pain,

How many years of her life,

Did she dedicate to that man.

The Gift

Something that will bring you to your knees.

Something that will bring you to complete silence.

Something that will make life worth living

Something that will take very air out of you

Something that will make you change your life.

Something that will bring out the best in you

Something that will nearly bring out the worst in you

Something very grand in life,

is the role of as a parent.

No Such Thing

Do yourself a favor and give it up.

Try walking the road of what's real,

Just sometimes.

Instead of dedicating your life

to pure luck.

Intergalactic Collision

If you apologized then that means

you'd have to acknowledge you were wrong

and face yourself.
Cowards go away from the truth,

the reality they created.
Everything you touch starts to die

with your poison of darkness.

You keep going to keep safely

seeking others' light.
We are all trapped

in the same world

of different realms.

What A Wonderful world

Death is painful,

Birth is so beautiful to the human.

One world

and time.

Lovers looking for forever's

Believers knowing never's

while here.

In betweener's saying whatever's.

What a test of time.

Wake Up

Why only I taste the uncertainty

in what all

others are fed.

And if resentment will kill me

then I'm already dead.

Snap to.

Smile too.

It's just another day

in the living dead.

Words is Bond

A promise is a promise,

Don't ruin it for the sake of speaking.

To keep them keeping into play,

With your lack of reasoning

If you really want to stay.

Because it comes a day

When the receiver begins to ignore

That precious mention

Which all of humanity

Should breath to adore.

We Are Poets

It's like a tornado of emotions trapped inside of you

You can never find the right words to speak

For all the many moments it desires to describe of each.

Every moment is unique

There's always a conversation

going on inside of you in "awe" of this world.

You live and feel in intense color

with your existence in slow motion

of moments mind scripting to each.

Of everything outside happening to you

and as time times with you,

I'm just on the clock of life,

With this ordained gift

and job to do.

Every answer found

creates a new question, endlessly.

I try to write it to describe it all,

The words scrambled most times

trapped inside of me.

An observer that never sleeps,

The life of a poet

ordained of me.

I Am My Brothers Keeper

When we all smile and laugh together

It feels like triumph in this world.

Remember that one laugh...

When one cries in pain,

We all ache in that pain,

But remind each other

there is purpose in everything.

Remember that one cry...

We can't fix it,

but we are all here.

We can love you no matter what,

Our love is always near.

No one lives forever,

but you will die knowing you were dear.

I AM

Can't look outside-

I am found.

I have to live from within.

Feels like everything against me.

I into this universe,

I push

and into the world

have to press back

so that it feels me.

It must know

And it knows I am here

I exist in

And claim this space.

It then respects me

Because I first acknowledged

and loved myself,

Valued my presence

And took that power

Of self

Into this world.

Awakened

Yesterday can do nothing for me now,

As I am thankful

I have been granted this new day,

Grateful for the now.

Shalom

It's not a dream I can see all the colors.

My life is beautiful.

All the colors are beautiful.

Love is beautiful.

The pain is beautiful.

My neighbor is beautiful.

The nations are beautiful.

Sometimes the wars are beautiful-

fighting the "disrupted" for our evolution's ultimate

peace,

vivid chaos to ultimate serenity.

Then elevated we are all together,

we go to elevate to a higher realm.

The eventual arrival in-time

to the resolved differences,

as one.

"As to the finale...

it may not be witnessed by you during your lifetime."

About the Author

Dr. Crystal Davison is a native to Houston, Tx where she currently resides.

She professionally practices as a pharmacist with a Doctoral degree in Pharmacology from Texas Southern University College of Pharmacy and Health Sciences.

Crystal writes books of poetry, spirituality, and self help/transformation which she believes is her true gift and passion in life.

These forms of her writing portray natural insight on day to day life of human life, thoughts, and emotions, which is so graciously depicted connecting to her readers. Crystal only desires that her poetry, writings, and self transformation tools be the light of others familiarity, pleasure, or even learning experiences in life which is captured.

Crystal is happily married and is a very proud mother.

More at

www.CrystalDavison.com

Davison Publishing

Thank You!

www.ingramcontent.com/pod-product-compliance
Lightning Source LLC
Chambersburg PA
CBHW071323130626
46556CB00004B/1719